Twist and Shout

★ Also by ★
Debbie Dadey

MERMAID TALES

Coming Soon

Mermaid Tales

Debbie Dadey

Illustrated by
Tatevik Avakyan

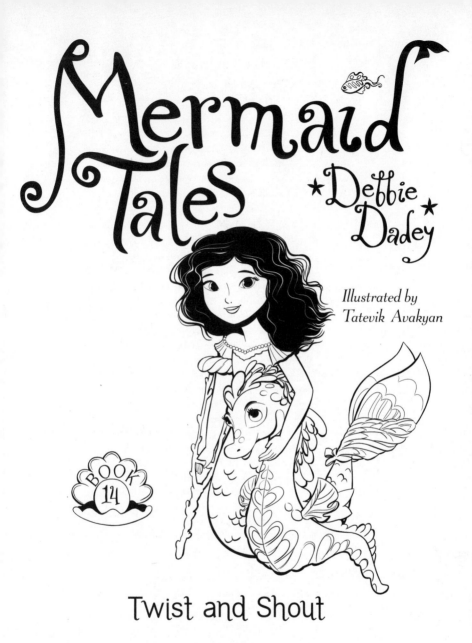

BOOK 14

Twist and Shout

ALADDIN
NEW YORK   LONDON   TORONTO   SYDNEY   NEW DELHI

ALADDIN

An imprint of Simon & Schuster Children's Publishing Division

1230 Avenue of the Americas, New York, NY 10020

This Aladdin hardcover edition May 2016

Text copyright © 2016 by Debbie Dadey

Illustrations copyright © 2016 by Tatevik Avakyan

Also available in an Aladdin paperback edition.

All rights reserved, including the right of reproduction in whole or in part in any form.

ALADDIN is a trademark of Simon & Schuster, Inc.,

and related logo is a registered trademark of Simon & Schuster, Inc.

For information about special discounts for bulk purchases,

please contact Simon & Schuster Special Sales at 1-866-506-1949

or business@simonandschuster.com.

The Simon & Schuster Speakers Bureau can bring authors to your live event.

For more information or to book an event contact the

Simon & Schuster Speakers Bureau at 1-866-248-3049

or visit our website at www.simonspeakers.com.

Series designed by Karin Paprocki

Jacket designed by Karina Granda

The text of this book was set in Belucian Book.

Manufactured in the United States of America 0416 FFG

2 4 6 8 10 9 7 5 3 1

Library of Congress Control Number 2015959474

ISBN 978-1-4814-4079-0 (hc)

ISBN 978-1-4814-4078-3 (pbk)

ISBN 978-1-4814-4080-6 (eBook)

To Betty Gibson and Judy Dohr

for helping me through

the worst week of my life

★ ★ ★ ★

Acknowledgments

Thanks to Metta and Michi Vojta for their keen eyes on the Mermaid Tales teaching units.

Cast of Characters

Shelly

Echo

Kiki

Pearl

Rocky

Contents

1

Sea Horses

GREAT JOB ON YOUR KELP reports," Mrs. Karp told her class of third graders. "I'm so glad you enjoyed 'My Side of the Ocean.' It is one of my favorite stories."

Echo tried to pay attention to the lesson, but she couldn't keep her pink tail from tapping the ocean floor. She couldn't wait until school was over! When the final conch shell sounded, Echo soared out of her seat and down the hallway of Trident Academy.

Her best friend, Shelly, followed Echo and patted her shoulder. "Do you have Tail Flippers practice today, or can you come over?"

Echo loved being part of the Tail Flippers dance team, and since the big Poseidon City Dance Competition was coming up next week, Coach Barnacle had been making them practice almost every day after school. Echo's fins ached from all the hard work.

Echo had been working especially hard

because she had a big job to do. She was going to perform a very difficult flip called a Scale Dropper. And she was going to do it from the top of a mer-pyramid formed by the other team members! It would be their big finale.

Normally, Echo would have spent her free afternoon at Shelly's home, especially since Shelly lived right above the Trident City People Museum. Echo loved learning about the human world. But there was something else she liked just as much: sea horses!

Echo shook her head. "We don't have practice today, but Rocky invited me to ride his sea horse this afternoon."

Shelly smiled. "That sounds fun."

★ 3 ★

Just then, Coach Barnacle swam by the mergirls. "Well, if it isn't our star Tail Flipper herself! Tell me, Echo, how is your Scale Dropper coming along?"

"Fin-tastic!" Echo told him. "I've even been waking up early to practice it every day before breakfast!"

"Mervelous!" Coach Barnacle boomed. "After all, you're our secret weapon! If you keep practicing, I think our team has a great chance of winning first place."

Coach Barnacle zoomed down the hall just as Rocky burst out of their classroom. He took one look at Echo and grinned. "Shake your tail! It's sea horse time!"

Echo squealed in delight. She waved good-bye to Shelly and sped out of Trident

Academy after Rocky. As they swam past the Big Rock Café, Echo's mouth watered at the smell of boxfish burgers. She'd love to have a snack, but she wanted to ride Pinky more.

Pinky was one of Rocky's two sea horses. Zollie was his first sea horse. Rocky's uncle had rescued Zollie from a human's net. Pinky was Zollie's mate, who'd come to stay at Rocky's house too. Echo couldn't help being a tiny bit jealous of Rocky. After all, he had two sea horses and she didn't have any. But at least Rocky was nice enough to let Echo ride Pinky.

The two merkids swam around Rocky's large home and a storage shell to find the two sea horses feeding on small shrimp.

When the pets saw Echo and Rocky, they raced over to see them. Echo laughed and hugged Pinky while Rocky petted Zollie's head. Soon the merkids were riding on the backs of Pinky and Zollie.

"This is shelltacular!" Rocky yelled. He leaned down over Zollie's orange neck, urging him to go faster.

Echo did the same to Pinky and yelled, "Giddyup!"

This is what it must be like to be a sailfish, Echo thought. She loved the feeling of water whipping through her curly black hair.

Pinky sprinted through MerPark. Echo waved when she passed Pearl, a girl from her class. Pearl frowned as the two sea horses charged past. "Echo Reef! You'd better slow that thing down!" Pearl snapped.

Echo laughed and shook her head at Pearl. "No wavy way!" Echo yelled. "This is too much fun!"

But just as Echo turned her head, something horrible happened!

Dr. Weedly

AMORAY EEL SLITHERED IN front of Pinky! The sea horse stopped suddenly, but Echo didn't. She went flying off Pinky's back and landed on a big rock with a *PLUNK*.

Pearl and Rocky rushed to Echo's side.

"Echo! Are you all right?" Rocky cried.

Pinky galloped over and licked Echo's face. "I'm not sure," Echo moaned. "My tail hurts!"

Pearl took charge. "Rocky, ring the dugong ambulance bell! Then get Echo's parents." The dugong's huge back would be able to carry Echo to the Trident City Medical Center.

Rocky's eyes grew wide, but he didn't move. He seemed to be frozen to the spot, staring at Echo.

"Go!" Pearl snapped at him. Rocky flipped his brown tail around and sped away.

"I'm scared," Echo told Pearl. "My tail looks like it's twisted."

"Don't worry. You'll be just fine," Pearl assured her.

Echo had an awful thought. "What about the Poseidon City Dance Competition?"

"Dr. Weedly will fix you right up," Pearl said, though she didn't sound very sure. "I bet you won't even miss one practice!"

Pearl held Echo's hand until the big dugong arrived. Soon after, Echo's parents showed up. The ambulance carried Echo to the medical center. Pearl and Rocky followed, but stayed in the waiting room. Pinky and Zollie peered through the window.

Echo's dad held one of her hands, while her mother held the other. Echo's tail felt like someone had twisted it into a tight knot. Dr. Weedly examined it carefully. He gently moved it up and down.

"Owww!" Echo yelped.

"Hmm," Dr. Weedly said, scribbling on a kelp pad. Finally he tapped his chin and frowned at Echo.

"I have some news," he announced. "But you're not going to like it."

No Dancing!

THE NEXT AFTERNOON ECHO sniffed the scurvy grass her mother had put in a vase beside her bed. The dainty white flowers did cheer up her hospital room, but Echo still felt glum. She kept hearing Doc Weedly's words in her head. "Your tail is twisted! Swimming and dancing are out of the question!"

A tear rolled down Echo's cheek just as three of her friends swept into the room.

"Echo!" Shelly said, giving her a hug. "It is so good to see you!"

Kiki nodded. "School wasn't the same without you."

"When are you coming back?" Pearl demanded. "We missed your Scale Dropper at Tail Flippers practice!"

Echo burst into tears. "Dr. Weedly said I can't dance. I can't even swim for a while!"

Shelly, Pearl, and Kiki gasped. "That's horrible," Kiki said softly. "I'm so sorry."

"I am going to start a petition to ban moray eels from Trident City!" Pearl snapped. "If that nasty eel hadn't slithered in front of you, none of this would have happened!"

Echo shook her head. "It's not the eel's fault! It was an accident."

"Wait a merminute," Shelly said. "Did the doctor say when you'd be able to swim?"

Echo looked at the big white bandage on her tail. "I have to keep my tail wrapped for a few days and then I can start swimming slowly."

Pearl squealed. "That's tail-kicking! If

you can swim in just a few days, then you can flip in a few days!"

Echo sighed. "But Dr. Weedly told me that it depends on how quickly my tail heals. There's a chance I won't be able to swim in time for the competition next week."

Pearl slapped her gold fins on the hospital room floor. "Nonsense! You'll be swimming and flipping in no time!"

Shelly frowned. "Pearl, Echo needs time to heal. Otherwise she could get even more hurt."

"But without her we won't win first place at the Poseidon City Dance Competition!" Pearl glared at Echo. "And that's not fair to the rest of the team."

Echo's heart sank. She didn't want to disappoint her teammates. Plus, she'd been working so hard on her Scale Dropper. There must be some way she could make her tail heal faster!

Crutchies to the Rescue!

TWO DAYS LATER KIKI AND Shelly were in MerPark after school. Pearl stopped beside them on her way home from Tail Flippers practice.

"What in the ocean are those?" Pearl asked Kiki. Shelly and Kiki each carried a long metal object that was wide on one end and narrow on the other.

"They're from the People Museum," Shelly explained. "Grandfather said humans use these when they hurt their legs. We thought they might help Echo."

"They're called crutchies," Kiki told Pearl.

"How do they work?" Pearl asked. "Will they help Echo flip faster? We really need her for the competition."

"That's the problem," Shelly said. "We don't have any idea how humans use them."

The three mergirls stared at the crutchies. "Maybe you use these holes to put your tailfins in and then someone pulls you along," Pearl suggested.

Shelly stuck one fin in each of the crutchies while her friends pulled on the short ends. *Splat!* Shelly fell facedown in the muddy ocean floor.

She sat up and wiped the mud from her face. "I'm pretty sure that's not right."

"What if we put them together to make a mini bed?" Kiki suggested.

Shelly and Pearl held the two crutchies side by side while Kiki sat on top. "It's working," Kiki said as her merfriends lifted her up. Unfortunately, the crutchies came apart and Kiki slammed to the ocean bottom.

"Ow," Kiki said, rubbing her own bottom. "That can't be right either."

"Maybe they're like flippers," Shelly said, grabbing a crutchie in each hand and flapping them up and down. She started rising in the water.

"That's it!" Pearl yelled. "Let's take them to Echo."

The girls rushed over to Echo's house. Echo was lying in her bed, looking at the latest issue of *MerStyle* magazine.

"Look what Grandpa Siren found," Shelly told Echo. "These are what humans use when they hurt their legs."

Echo sat up and smiled. "Really?" She was excited to try something that a real person might have used.

"Give me those," Pearl said, snatching the crutchies away from Shelly. "This is how you use them."

Pearl flapped her arms up and down while holding the crutchies. Unfortunately, they whacked Echo's barrel sponge chair and toppled an antique hawksbill turtle shell lamp.

"What are you mergirls doing?" Echo's older sister, Crystal, asked as she floated into the room.

"Sorry about the mess," Kiki said, picking up the lamp. "We were just showing Kiki how to use crutchies."

Crystal took one look at Pearl and laughed. "That's not how you use those," Crystal said.

"How do you know?" Pearl asked.

"Because in my sixth-grade human study class we learned about them," Crystal said matter-of-factly. "And they're called crutches, not crutchies." She grabbed them from Pearl, tucked one under each armpit, and swung her tail between them. She zipped across Echo's bedroom in just a few seconds.

"Wow!" Echo said. "That's amazing."

"Totally wavy," Shelly agreed. "With those, you can be back in school tomorrow."

Echo smiled. She had actually missed being with her friends at Trident Academy.

"And you'll be doing the Scale Dropper before you know it," Pearl said, nodding her head.

Crystal frowned at Pearl. "That's not going to happen," Crystal said. "Echo needs to forget all about that silly competition and focus on getting well."

"It's not a silly competition!" Echo insisted. But the truth was clear: Unless there was some sort of a miracle, there was no way she could tail-flip in the Poseidon City Dance Competition.

5

Miracle?

I T TOOK ECHO THREE TIMES AS
long to get to school the next morning using the crutches. It was a good
thing she had left extra early.

Shelly was a true friend. She floated
beside Echo the whole way. "Sorry I'm so
slow," Echo told her. "Using these really

makes you appreciate how fast swim-ming is."

"No worries," Shelly said. "If we'd been going fast I wouldn't have noticed those pretty mandarin fish." She pointed to a group of brightly colored fish. Each one was orange and yellow with blue and green markings.

Echo looked up from her crutches and smiled. "That's true. Normally we would have zoomed right past them. And look at that stargazer in the mud there."

"Oh, be careful. Don't let it sting your fin," Shelly warned.

Echo agreed. "My tail is sore enough without that!"

Just as they arrived at Trident Academy,

Pearl rushed up to greet them. "Echo! All our worries are over," Pearl proclaimed, holding up a glass bottle.

"What's that?" Echo asked, peering at the bright-blue blob inside the bottle.

"It's miracle cream," Pearl explained. "I found it on my mother's dresser. The bottle says it will fix any skin problem."

Shelly shook her head. "I'm pretty sure that won't help Echo."

Pearl frowned. "Of course it will. I happen to know this is very expensive stuff. It's made from the webbing of the blue-footed booby."

Echo gasped. "They hurt a bird to make it?"

"No, of course not." Pearl shook her

head and pointed to the tiny print on the bottle. "No birds were injured in the making of this product."

Echo felt relieved, but she still wasn't sure she should use something that cost so much money. "Won't your mom be upset?"

"Not at all," Pearl said, opening the

bottle. "She's always happy to help someone in need."

Echo had to admit she really did need to get well fast. She used the crutches to move to a bench in front of Trident Academy. With Pearl and Shelly's help, she unwrapped the big bandage on her tail.

Echo giggled as Pearl slathered the cream on her fins and tail. "That tickles," Echo said.

Pearl smiled as she used every last bit of the miracle cream. "I bet that means it's working."

Echo liked the tingling feeling in her tail. It felt good later as Mrs. Karp's class welcomed her back.

"Hello, three-tail girl," Rocky said.

"What are you talking about? I only have one tail, and it feels just great," Echo told him.

"You have one broken tail and two metal ones," he teased, pointing to the crutches. Rocky's kidding didn't bother Echo because Pearl's cream had made her fins feel so sparkling good.

But as the morning went on, the tingling feeling stopped. When Echo used her crutches to get to the cafeteria, her tail began to prickle, then itch, then burn.

"My tail is on fire!" she cried.

6

Dilly Dally DoDo

ECHO HAD NEVER BEEN TO
the Trident Academy nurse's
office before, and she was
really scared. Her tail felt like she'd
bumped into a weever fish, but when
Echo saw the nurse, she forgot about the
pain for a mersecond.

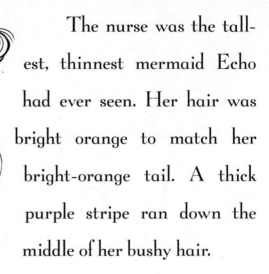

The nurse was the tall-
est, thinnest mermaid Echo
had ever seen. Her hair was
bright orange to match her
bright-orange tail. A thick
purple stripe ran down the
middle of her bushy hair.

"Well, well," the nurse said.
"What's my patient's name?"

"Echo," Echo squeaked.

"Shelltacular! My name is Dilly Dally
DoDo, but you can call me Nurse DoDo."

"Is that your real name?" Echo asked in
surprise.

Dilly Dally DoDo laughed. "Do you
think I would make up such a name? My
parents were a bit silly."

Echo nodded. She'd always thought it would be fun to have an unusual name, but not one as wild as Dilly Dally DoDo!

"Now, let's take a look at this tail." Nurse DoDo gently unwrapped Echo's bandage.

"I hurt it by falling off a sea horse," Echo explained. "But this morning my friend Pearl gave me some miracle cream to help it heal faster."

"That was a bad idea," Nurse DoDo said. "I think it was a disaster cream, not a miracle cream. You must be allergic to it."

"Oh no!" Echo said when she saw her tail. Her lovely pink tail had turned a yucky shade of green! Echo's eyes watered and she knew she was going to cry.

"Don't worry," Nurse DoDo said. "I

think you'll be fine once we wash all this goop off."

As Nurse DoDo began wiping off the miracle cream, she asked, "What did the sea say to the little mergirl?"

Echo shrugged and Nurse DoDo answered, "Nothing, it just waved."

Echo giggled.

"How many tickles does it take to make an octopus laugh?" Nurse DoDo asked as she continued cleaning Echo's tail.

Echo guessed, "Eight? One for each arm?"

Nurse DoDo shook her head. "Nope, ten-tacles!"

Echo laughed. She knew that an octopus's arms were called tentacles.

Echo was glad to see her tail returning to its normal color. The stinging had already stopped. "Is there a secret to helping my tail get better?" Echo asked.

Nurse DoDo smiled. "Of course." She leaned in and whispered something into Echo's ear.

Another Plan

ARE YOU ALL RIGHT?" MRS. Karp asked when Echo got back to class.

"Yes," Echo said. "Nurse Dilly Dally DoDo made me feel fin-tastic." Echo noticed that Rocky laughed at the unusual

name, but Mrs. Karp gave him a look that silenced him.

"What happened?" Shelly whispered as Mrs. Karp began a lesson on eels. Kiki and Pearl leaned in to listen.

"I was allergic to that miracle cream," Echo told her friends.

Pearl twisted her pearl necklace in her hands. "I'm so sorry," she whispered.

"It's okay," Echo said. She knew Pearl had been trying to help, but maybe Dilly Dally DoDo's secret was the only way to heal: plenty of rest. It didn't seem like much of a secret, though. Echo sighed and tried to pay attention to Mrs. Karp.

"Who can name an eel that can change colors?" Mrs. Karp asked.

Kiki raised her hand. "A ribbon eel?"

"Yes, you may have seen some at the coral reef next to the Plaza Hotel," Mrs. Karp told them. "Now, who knows which eel can swallow a fish that's as big as it is?"

Echo was pretty sure that was a gulper eel, but she didn't raise her hand. Instead she stared at the fresh bandage the nurse had put on her tail. Echo wished that the cream *had* worked a miracle, but when she moved her tail, it still hurt.

Surely Echo wasn't the first mermaid to ever injure her tail. What did other mermaids do? Did they just wait to get better? Or did they try to heal faster? Echo didn't know what to do.

Just then Pearl leaned over and tapped

Echo on the shoulder. "Meet me after school," Pearl hissed. "I have another plan."

Echo shook her head. Pearl's last scheme had sent Echo to the nurse's office with a horrible green tail. She wasn't taking any more chances!

Echo didn't want to hurt Pearl's feelings, but she was going to follow Nurse Dilly Dally DoDo's advice. She knew she had to stay as far away from Pearl as possible!

Accidents Happen

AFTER SCHOOL ECHO GOT on her crutches and, with Shelly's help, managed to steer clear of the statues and a prickly redfish in MerPark. But she almost fell when Rocky splashed to a stop right in front of her.

"Watch out!" Echo said. "You almost knocked me down."

"I wanted to tell you something," he said. But he didn't say anything. Instead, he stared down at the ocean floor. Pearl swam up beside them.

"Echo, you have to listen to my idea!" Pearl snapped. "It's mervelous!"

"It'll have to wait," Echo said. "Rocky wants to talk to me first."

Pearl stared at Rocky. "For shark's sake then, spit it out!"

Rocky scratched his brown tail before finally blurting, "Echo, I'm sorry. If it wasn't for me, you wouldn't have gotten hurt."

Pearl nodded. "That's right.

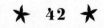

★ 42 ★

You and those silly sea horses of yours caused this mess."

"Pearl!" Shelly said in surprise.

Echo frowned at Pearl. "You shouldn't say things like that."

"Well, it's the truth," Pearl said. "If you don't get well in time for the competition, it will be all because of them."

"What about you, Pearl?" Rocky asked. "If you hadn't distracted Echo, none of this would have happened."

"That's not true," Echo told them. After all, she'd been going too fast to be safe. "It's no one's fault."

Rocky shrugged. "Zollie and Pinky feel just awful."

Suddenly Echo realized that while she'd

been feeling sorry for herself, Zollie and Pinky were probably feeling just as bad. She needed to let them know that the accident wasn't their fault.

"I have to go," Echo said.

"But you still haven't heard my plan!" Pearl cried.

Echo didn't wait to listen to Pearl. She moved along the ocean floor as fast as her crutches would let her. Pearl swam away in a huff, but Shelly and Rocky followed Echo, occasionally swimming forward to move a dragonfish or a balloon fish out of Echo's way.

By the time they got to Rocky's big shell at the edge of Trident City, Echo was moving quickly. Rocky led the way to the back of his home. Echo came next on her crutches. Shelly swam behind, in case Echo needed help.

Zollie and Pinky snorted when they saw Echo. She broke into a big smile as Pinky hurried over to her.

"Hi, Pinky," Echo said. "I just wanted you to know that my accident wasn't your fault."

Pinky nuzzled her snout against Echo's cheek. "It wasn't anyone's fault," Echo said, looking at Zollie. "Sometimes accidents just happen."

Zollie dashed over, and Echo patted him on the head. "I'm so lucky to have you two for friends," Echo told the sea horses.

Zollie and Pinky neighed in agreement. Echo laughed, but then she remembered Pearl. Echo was curious. What did Pearl have up her sleeve now?

Human Games

AT HOME THAT AFTERNOON, Echo sank into her purple sea-fan bed. She couldn't remember ever being so tired. Her arms were sore from using the crutches to move. It was a good tired, because she was happy that she'd been able to go to school, as well as see Pinky and Zollie. The day would have been perfect if she'd been able to go to Tail Flippers practice.

A tear slid down Echo's cheek. If it hadn't been for the accident, she would have been the star of the competition. Now she'd be lucky if Coach Barnacle didn't kick her off the team. After all, who knew when she'd be able to flip again? There were plenty of other mergirls who'd love to take her place.

She gazed down at the stack of get-well cards her classmates had made for her. It made her feel better that her friends cared so much.

AFTER DINNER, SHELLY AND KIKI SWAM into Echo's room. "Thanks for the get-well cards," Echo told her merfriends.

Kiki smiled. "We're just glad you're feeling better."

"Want to play a game?" Shelly asked.

"It's a human one Shelly's grandfather let us borrow from the People Museum," Kiki explained.

Echo squealed. "That sounds fun. How do you play?"

Shelly put a flat marble square on Kiki's bed. It was divided into smaller squares that were black and white. Then Kiki put lots of small statues on the marble board. A few of the statues looked like sea horses.

"This game is called Race to the Castle," Shelly explained. "We take turns trying to

get to the opposite side of the board. First one there wins."

Kiki nodded. "We can play in teams if Crystal will join us."

Echo smiled at her friends as Shelly explained the rules. Echo still wished she hadn't twisted her tail, but having good friends made being hurt a whole lot easier.

10

Shake Your Tail

"H EY, ECHO!" ROCKY YELLED the next morning in Mer-Park. Shelly and Echo were on their way to school. Echo stopped and waved at Rocky.

"Can I try out your crutches?" he asked.

Shelly shook her head. "I don't think that's such a good idea."

"Aw, it'll be fun," Rocky said.

Echo shrugged. "I don't mind." She pointed to a marble bench near the statue of Poseidon. "Help me onto that bench."

In two merminutes, Shelly and Echo were laughing with Rocky. He was having a terrible time making the crutches work. Twice he had to spit out sand dollars that accidentally floated into his mouth. He kept turning in circles and almost ran into the statue of Mapella.

"This is a lot harder than it looks," Rocky said with a laugh. "But it's kind of fun."

Echo nodded and wiped a tear of laughter from her eye. It had taken her a while to get the hang of the crutches too.

Pearl swam by. "You'd better bubble down and get to school, or you'll be late," she told them.

"Gotta shake my tail," Rocky said, quickly giving Echo her crutches and swimming away. "Mrs. Karp said I'd be in big trouble if I'm late one more time."

Pearl stopped long enough to point her finger at Echo. "And *you* had better come to Tail Flippers practice after school," Pearl said.

"Why? Echo still can't flip," Shelly argued. "Her tail isn't healed yet."

"But she won't even listen to my plan!" Pearl growled. "Echo, I don't think you care about the Tail Flippers!"

"Of course I do!" Echo said.

Pearl lifted her nose in the water with a sniff. "Then prove it. At least come to practice to cheer us on. And if you're lucky, I'll tell you my big idea."

"Okay, okay," Echo said. "What is your big idea?"

Pearl flipped her long blond hair around and swam away, calling over her shoulder, "No wavy way! You'll have to come to practice to find out!"

Pearl's Big Idea

I'D BETTER GET TO TAIL FLIPPERS practice or Pearl will be *flipping mad!* Echo thought when the last conch sounded to end the school day. She was amazed at how quickly she got to the practice field using her crutches.

"Yay! You made it!" shouted the Tail

Flippers. They surrounded Echo. Even Coach Barnacle swam over to greet her.

"I won't be able to dance for a while," Echo explained to Coach Barnacle. "I'll understand if you want to give my spot to someone else."

Coach Barnacle threw his hands up in the air. "No wavy way! You are our best flipper! We'll figure out a way to make things work until you can flip again."

Echo couldn't believe Coach Barnacle was being so nice to her after she'd ruined their chances for the big upcoming competition. She decided she'd do her best to cheer them to victory anyway. She sat down on the nearest bench to watch.

But before practice began, Coach Barnacle and the mergirls floated into a circle. Pearl was at the center, and Echo could tell that everyone was listening carefully. Every once in a while, someone would look at Echo and smile. What were they doing?

Finally Pearl swam over with her hands on her hips. "Why are you sitting down?" she asked Echo.

"If I can't flip, then I'm going to cheer you guys to victory," Echo said.

"Oh no, you're not," Pearl said.

Echo's heart sank. Had they decided to kick her off the Tail Flippers after all? "But Coach Barnacle said he'd figure out a way for me to stay on the team," she said with a gulp.

Pearl shook her head. With a big sigh, Echo got up and used her crutches to move slowly off the kelp field.

"Where are you going?" Pearl asked.

"I'm leaving," Echo said sadly. "Good luck at the competition."

Pearl grabbed Echo by the arm. "You're not going anywhere," Pearl

said. "I was just telling everyone my big idea, and guess what?"

"What?" Echo asked.

Pearl grinned. "They loved it!"

Echo shrugged. "That's fin-tastic, but what does it have to do with me?"

"Because," Pearl said, "you and your crutches *are* the big idea."

"What you are you talking about?" Echo asked.

"I'll explain in a second. But first, come on," Pearl said. "We have a lot of work to do. The competition is in three days!"

The Competition

ECHO POPPED OPEN HER eyes and threw off her kelp covers. It was the morning of the competition. Was her tail healed? Dr. Weedly had told her not to wear the bandage anymore, so Echo wiggled her fins carefully. They didn't hurt!

Slowly she spun her tail in a circle. Ouch! That was painful!

But there was still hope. If Pearl's big idea worked, she could be in the competition even with an injured tail.

Pearl's plan with the miracle cream had been a disaster, though. Would this be just as awful?

Echo got out of bed, put on her uniform, and grabbed her crutches. Crystal met her in the kitchen. "Ta-da!" Crystal said. "I made you a special breakfast!"

"Thanks," Echo said. She was almost too nervous to eat, but she didn't want to hurt her sister's feelings. So Echo ate a big shell bowl full of sea hare sausage and sea rose eggs.

"Your uniform looks great!" Crystal said, and put her hand on Echo's shoulder. "I know you feel bad about not being in the competition, but your tail will be perfect before you know it! And there are plenty of other contests in your future."

Echo nodded. She hadn't told her family about Pearl's big idea. After all, what if it didn't work out?

As soon as Echo brushed her hair with a Venus comb and put some sparkling plankton in her hair, it was time to leave for the competition. Coach Barnacle had arranged for a manta ray to take the Tail Flippers to Poseidon Prep School.

Crystal, Echo, and their parents all boarded the huge manta together. It was already loaded with the other members of the team and the pep band. Pearl was sitting in the middle of the manta with her mother. They waved and Echo waved back. Every member of the Tail Flippers team wore their uniform of bright gold.

"This is exciting," Crystal told Echo, giving her hand a squeeze.

"I'm so proud of you for supporting your team even if you can't compete with them," Echo's mother said. Echo nodded, but inside her stomach was doing all kind of flips. She just wished her tail could do flips too!

When they finally arrived at Poseidon Prep, Echo was so scared, she felt like she might throw up. "Are you ready?" Pearl asked, swimming up beside her.

Echo shook her head. "Are you sure this is a good idea?"

Pearl surprised Echo by saying, "Don't worry about it. If it doesn't work perfectly, then at least we tried."

Echo smiled. "Okay! Let's bubble down and do it!"

An announcer came onto the loud-speaker. "Welcome to the eleventh annual Poseidon City Dance Competition!" The Trident Academy team clapped as the performing schools were announced.

The competition began. Ten teams from all over the Western Oceans were performing. After the Bubbles School took their bows, Echo whispered to Pearl, "They're really good!"

"But they don't have you," Pearl replied.

When the Trident Academy Pep Band starting banging on their sharkskin drums and blowing on their conch-shell horns, Echo was ready. She took her place on the stage alongside her teammates.

The Tail Flippers flipped around her in a rainbow of tails as Echo kept time by tapping on the floor with her crutches. Echo's heart soared as her merfriends lifted her up. She held her crutches high in the air as they spun her around and around. The whole team whirled with her and then let go. Pearl soared to the top of the gym as the rest of the Tail Flippers did triple backflips. They then helped Echo gently float down to the floor. She landed crutches first with her tail straight up in the water. When they finished, the crowd cheered. Echo could see the surprised looks on her parents' faces as they clapped. Crystal yelled, "Go Echo!"

As the Tail Flippers sailed off the floor, Coach Barnacle congratulated them. "Merladies, that was tails-down your best performance yet!"

Echo smiled. Even though she wished she could have flipped, she was happy that she'd had the chance to perform with her friends.

Next, Poseidon Prep's team spun onto the stage. Their costumes sparkled like silver allis shad fish, and from the serious looks on their faces, Echo could tell they really wanted to win.

"All right, begin!" yelled the tallest flipper. Immediately, Poseidon Prep flipped in a circle to a loud thumping beat. It was hard to know where to look because everyone seemed to be doing something different.

After the other schools had performed, it was time for the awards. Echo was so nervous she wanted to disappear into the floor like a sand bubbler crab.

The headmaster of Poseidon Prep School floated up to a podium. "Everyone did a wonderful job today. Let's give a big fin clap to all the teams."

Echo very carefully tapped her fins together. They were still a bit sore, but at least she didn't have to wear the big tail bandage anymore.

"And now, for the third-place winner . . ."

Echo held her breath.

"Poseidon Prep School!" the headmaster announced.

The squad from Poseidon Prep swam up to their headmaster and accepted a big bronze urn with a number three on the side. Echo was surprised they had come in third. They had flipped so high! If Poseidon Prep had gotten third place, there was no hope that the Trident Academy Tail Flippers could win.

"And now, for the second-place team," the headmaster went on.

Echo gently crossed her tail fins.

"Trident Academy Tail Flippers!" the headmaster announced.

Echo and Pearl looked at each other and squealed. The entire Trident Academy team swam up to the stage—except for Echo, who used her crutches. The Poseidon Prep headmaster presented Coach Barnacle with a silver urn that had a huge 2 on the side. Echo thought she'd never seen anything so beautiful in her life.

"Here," Coach said, handing the prize to Echo. "This is for you. Without your crutches, we never would have won second place."

Echo smiled. She wasn't sure that was true. "Don't forget it was Pearl's idea," Echo told him.

"Hey," Pearl said with a wink. "It was teamwork."

Echo wanted more than anything to do a flip to celebrate. "Will you do a flip for me?" she asked Pearl.

Pearl did a three-point spin and a half-twist flip.

"Hurrah for the Tail Flippers!" Echo cheered.

Class Cards for Echo

✦ ✦ ✦

Dear Echo,
I am so sorry you hurt your tail, and I hope you get well really soon. Mrs. Karp has us learning about eels since an eel swam in front of your sea horse. I think the slender snipe eel is pretty cool. It looks like a skinny snake with a smile.
Your friend,
Shelly

Dear Echo,
I am sorry that an old moray eel caused you to get hurt. I'm also sorry that Mrs. Karp is making us study eels. Can you believe the conger eel lays three million eggs?
Signed,
Rocky

Dear Echo,
I still think we should get a petition together to get rid of all the chain moray eels in Trident City. And what about those European eels? I don't like their pointy snouts. Yuck! Oh, get well soon.
Your fellow Tail Flipper,
Pearl

Dear Echo,
I hope you are feeling much better. I was very worried about you. I know being in the Tail Flippers competition means a lot to you, so I hope it works out. Mrs. Karp told us about the spotted garden eel. I like how they live together in a group and stick up out of the sand.
Your friend,
Kiki

The Mermaid Song

REFRAIN:

Let the water roar

Deep down we're swimming along

Twirling, swirling, singing the mermaid song.

VERSE 1:

Shelly flips her tail

Racing, diving, chasing a whale

Twirling, swirling, singing the mermaid song.

VERSE 2:

Pearl likes to shine

Oh my Neptune, she looks so fine

Twirling, swirling, singing the mermaid song.

VERSE 3:

Shining Echo flips her tail

Backward and forward without fail

Twirling, swirling, singing the mermaid song.

VERSE 4:

Amazing Kiki

Far from home and floating so free

Twirling, swirling, singing the mermaid song.

Author's Note

MERMAIDS COME IN all sizes, colors, and shapes, but very few mermaids can't swim. I was proud of Echo's friends when they helped her find a way to get to school. Especially surprising was the way Pearl came up with a big idea to save the day! Sometimes Pearl thinks only of herself, so I was glad this time she helped her whole team. I hope we can all be like that for our friends and help them out when they need us.

Swim free and visit me at:

www.debbiedadey.com

Debbie Dadey

Glossary

ALLIS SHAD: The allis shad is a herring that is also called the May fish. In April or May it leaves the ocean to swim into rivers to lay eggs.

BALLOON FISH: This fish, also known as the spiny porcupine fish, can grow to three times its normal size by taking in water or air.

BARNACLE: These crustaceans attach to rocks and even ships.

BARREL SPONGE: This sponge has been known to get quite large but has a hard surface.

BLUE-FOOTED BOOBY: This water bird lives on the rocky coasts of islands and hunts for fish in the water. The adults have bright turquoise-blue feet.

BOXFISH: The yellow boxfish is rather square shaped. When it is scared, it can release poison through its skin into the water around it.

CHAIN MORAY EEL: Most moray eels can survive out of water for short periods of time, as long as their skin stays wet.

CONCH: This large sea snail has one of the most beautiful shells of any ocean creature.

CONGER EEL: This big gray eel has probably scared many treasure hunters. It likes to stick its head out of holes and crevices in wrecked ships and reefs.

CORAL: Some tiny corals work together to build huge coral reefs.

DRAGONFISH: This deep-sea fish is small but has very large teeth. Like many deep-sea fish, it can glow!

DUGONG: The dugong looks a lot like a manatee. It lives on the ocean floor, grazing in sea-grass beds.

DUMBO OCTOPUS: Dumbo octopi live in the deep sea and have very large fins that look like ears.

EUROPEAN EEL: This eel swims thousands of miles to lay its eggs.

GULPER EEL: This fish has a small head and little eyes with a huge mouth and enormous jaws.

HAWKSBILL SEA TURTLE: The hawksbill sea turtle shell is the chief source of tortoiseshell, which is often collected for its beauty. Mermaids, however, have learned to use only shells from turtles that have died naturally.

KELP: Kelp is the large brown seaweed that grows in underwater forests.

MANDARIN FISH: The mandarin fish is one of the most colorful of all reef fish; however, its skin is covered with slime!

MANTA RAY: One of the giants of the sea, manta rays can be twenty-three feet wide, which is longer than a car.

PLANKTON: Plankton are the tiny creatures that many ocean animals, such as whales, use for food.

PRICKLY REDFISH: This sea cucumber crawls along the ocean floor. It looks like a big shaggy mop!

RIBBON EEL: Ribbon eels like to hide in the cracks in a coral reef.

SAILFISH: The sailfish is the fastest fish in the ocean. It can keep the same pace as the fastest land animal, the cheetah, which can run seventy miles per hour!

SAND BUBBLER CRAB: If you see hundreds of perfectly formed balls of sand on the shore, chances are tiny one-inch sand bubbler crabs are around. These crabs make sand balls while gathering small bits of food. One crab can make twelve balls in a minute.

SAND DOLLAR: The flat, round sand dollar is actually a type of sea urchin.

SCURVY GRASS: Scurvy grass grows along the shore. Its thick green leaves were once eaten to prevent a disease called scurvy.

SEA FAN: Sea fans are sometimes called sea whips. They anchor themselves in sand or mud. Most are nocturnal, which means they are awake at night.

SEA HARE: The sea hare is a type of sea slug, but its tentacles stick up to make it look like a rabbit or hare.

SEA HORSE: Sea horses are fish, but they are bad swimmers! They prefer to hold on to coral or seaweed to stay in one place.

SEA ROSE: A sea creature called a Spanish dancer makes egg ribbons that look very much like a beautiful red rose.

SLENDER SNIPE EEL: This long, thin eel has jaws shaped like a bird's bill. Because of the way the ends are turned out, it can never close its mouth!

SPOTTED GARDEN EEL: This tiny eel looks like a flower sprouting up from the ocean floor.

STARGAZER: The common stargazer looks like a mix of a bulldog and a seal! This fish likes to lie partly buried in the sand.

VENUS COMB: This sea snail has a shell that looks a lot like a comb.

WEEVER FISH: This brown fish likes to bury itself partly in the sand around the English shoreline. But beware—if you step on one, it will hurt!

FIND OUT WHAT HAPPENS IN THE NEXT . . .

Mermaid Tales

★ Debbie Dadey ★

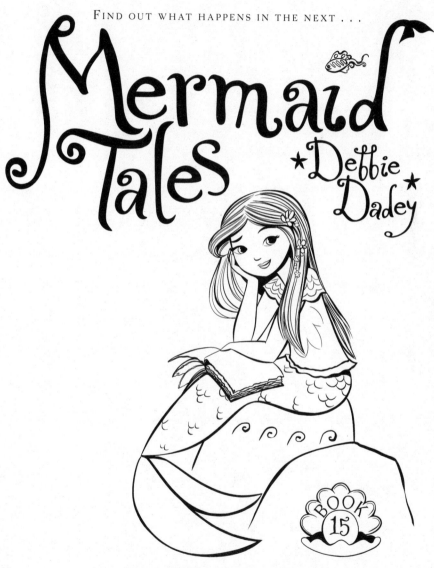

BOOK 15

Books vs. Looks

A Special Letter

KIKI CORAL WAS SWIMMING to her dorm room after school one Friday when she felt a tap on her shoulder.

"Miss Coral," Madame Hippocampus announced. "You have a letter."

"Thanks," Kiki said as Madame handed

her a kelp envelope. Kiki smiled as she raced down the hallway toward her Trident Academy dorm room. She nearly bumped into a mergirl from her third-grade class.

"Watch out, for shark's sake!" Pearl Swamp snapped.

"Sorry," Kiki said, still clutching her letter. Her heart pounded in excitement. Kiki loved getting notes from her family in the Eastern Oceans. It made going to school so far away, in the Western Oceans, a little easier.

She soared through her doorway and swam straight to her killer-whale skeleton bed. Once she had curled her purple tail among the gray heron feathers, Kiki ripped open the letter.

Dear Kiki,

Hi! How is school? I wish I could go 2 Trident 2.

Guess what? My friends started a book club! We are reading a scary book. I will show it 2 u when u get home!

Miss u,

Yuta

Kiki read the letter twice and blinked back a tear. Her brother Yuta was a year younger than she was. She had been very close to him ever since they were small fry. Now that she went to school so far away, she really missed him.

Kiki glanced around her dorm room. Rainbow-colored jellyfish lamps hung from the curved ceiling, and a small waterfall tinkled gently in a corner. One whole wall glittered with plankton. A magnificent coral reef made up another wall. Kiki knew she was lucky to have such a fin-tastic space all to herself. At home her brothers had to share bedrooms.

But living all by herself could be lonely. Sometimes she wished she had someone to talk to. Fridays were the worst, because her best friends, Echo and Shelly, usually spent Friday evenings with their families. Many students who lived in the dorms also left to visit relatives.

At least she had plenty of books to read! Kiki looked at her tall rock bookcase and smiled. She had read every book on her shelf again and again. Reading stories always helped Kiki feel less lonesome.

Kiki read Yuta's letter one more time before jumping up and down with excitement. Even though Yuta was far away, he had given her a mer-velous idea!

Dr. Bottom

THE FOLLOWING MONDAY, Kiki couldn't wait to tell her merfriends about her idea. She had read in a book that humans had a device that allowed them to talk to people far away. Kiki wished she had one of those.

"Where are they?" Kiki tapped her purple tail on the classroom floor. If Shelly and Echo didn't swim in soon, they would be tardy. Their teacher, Mrs. Karp, was already at the front of the class. Just as the conch sounded to start the school day, Shelly, Echo, and a merboy named Rocky swooshed into the room.

Mrs. Karp raised a green eyebrow at the almost-late arrivals before starting her lesson. "Class, today we will start a new area of study. Who can tell me about symbiosis?"

"I know! I know!" Rocky called out. "That's where you bang two shiny things together to make a really loud noise."

"Not quite," Mrs. Karp said. "Symbiosis

is when two different creatures live together in the same environment."

Kiki raised her hand. She remembered her father talking about that last year, before she had come to Trident Academy. "Don't the clownfish and the anemone do that?"

Mrs. Karp smiled and slapped her white tail on the classroom floor. "That's exactly right. And each one helps the other. The clownfish gets a safe home, and in return it cleans the anemone and even makes waste for it to eat. This is called mutualism."

Pearl gagged and twisted her pearl necklace. "That's disgusting!"

Mrs. Karp shrugged. "That's science. Today we have a special guest who will tell us more about different symbiotic relationships. Students, please welcome Dr. Bottom." Kiki knew that Dr. Bottom usually taught fourth grade, but he sometimes switched with other teachers to teach science, his favorite subject.

"Good morning, Dr. Bottom," the merstudents said together. Rocky snickered when he said the science teacher's last name, but a quick look from Mrs. Karp silenced him.

"GOOD MORNING, CLASS!" Dr. Bottom shouted.

Kiki almost fell out of her chair. She quickly figured out that Dr. Bottom was hard of hearing. Over the next two hours he screamed his lesson about three different types of symbiotic relationships: mutualism, commensalism, and parasitism. Kiki tried to pay attention, but her mind kept wandering to her great idea.

When Dr. Bottom was finally finished, Kiki raced to the cafeteria for lunch. She hoped her friends would love her idea too.

Debbie Dadey

is the author and coauthor of more than one hundred and sixty children's books, including the series The Adventures of the Bailey School Kids. A former teacher and librarian, Debbie and her family live in Sevierville, Tennessee. She hopes you'll visit www.debbiedadey.com for lots of mermaid fun.